DATE DUE

Our American Family™

I Am
Jewish
American

Elizabeth Weitzman

The Rosen Publishing Group's
PowerKids Press™
New York

For my grandmother

Published in 1997 by The Rosen Publishing Group, Inc.
29 East 21st Street, New York, NY 10010

First Edition

Book Design: Erin McKenna

Photo Credits: Cover © Rob Goldman/FPG International Corp.; photo illustration © Icon Comm./FPG International Corp.; p. 4 © John Michael/International Stock Photography; pp. 7, 8, 11 © FPG International Corp.; p. 12 © F. Sieb/H. Armstrong Roberts, Inc.; p. 15 © Zefa-U.K./H. Armstrong Roberts, Inc.; p. 16 © D. Campione/H. Armstrong Roberts, Inc.; p. 19 © Michael P. Manheim/International Stock Photography; p. 20 © Jerry Finberg/FPG International Corp.

Weitzman, Elizabeth.
   I Am Jewish American / by Elizabeth Weitzman.
      p.   cm. — (Our American family)
  Includes index.
  Summary: A Jewish American girl discusses her faith, traditions, heritage, food, history, and pride in her identity.
  ISBN 0-8239-5006-9
  1. Jews—United States—Juvenile literature. [1. Jews—United States.] I. Title. II. Series.
E184.J5S87818 1997
973'.04924—dc21
                                            97-3584
                                           CIP
                                         AC

Manufactured in the United States of America

Contents

1 Rachel   5

2 A Journey to a New Country   6

3 Ellis Island   9

4 The Lower East Side   10

5 Shabbat   13

6 Synagogue   14

7 Food   17

8 Israel   18

9 Bat Mitzvah   21

10 I Am Jewish American   22

Glossary   23

Index   24

Rachel

Hi! My name is Rachel. I live in Chicago with my parents and my sister, Lauren. My family is Jewish. Our religion is **Judaism** (JOO-day-izm). My Grandma Lena came to America from Russia when she was seven years old. Life was very hard for her family in Russia because they were part of a **minority** (my-NOR-ih-tee). That means they were different from most of the others around them. Most Russians weren't Jewish. Many people in Russia didn't think anyone, including my grandma's family, should be able to practice Judaism.

◀ Family is very important to Jewish Americans.

A Journey to a New Country

When my great-grandparents found out they could leave Russia, they were very happy. Like many other **immigrants** (IM-uh-grents), they took a boat to America. The ride over was very hard. People were crowded together and there wasn't much food. Many people got sick. But they all knew it would be worth the trouble. They were going to the United States, a country where they would be free to practice any religion and follow any **traditions** (truh-DISH-unz) they liked.

When they came to America, immigrants brought only as much as they could carry. ▶

6

Ellis Island

The boat that brought Grandma Lena to America landed on Ellis Island in New York. She says that the first thing she saw was the Statue of Liberty. She also saw more people than she ever had before. Between 1892 and 1924, millions of immigrants came to Ellis Island from Ireland, Italy, Russia, and many other countries. Grandma and her parents spoke a language called **Yiddish** (YID-ish). They didn't speak any English at all. Luckily, they had an American cousin who came to Ellis Island to meet them.

◀ Nearly all immigrants who passed through Ellis Island went on to become American citizens.

The Lower East Side

Like thousands of other Jewish immigrants, Grandma and her parents went straight from Ellis Island to an area of New York City called the Lower East Side. They moved into a tiny apartment with their cousin's family. There were two rooms for seven people. The crowded building they lived in was called a tenement. After a few weeks, my great-grandfather found a job as a shoemaker. Grandma Lena went to school right away so she could start learning the language and history of her new country.

Even though their homes were crowded, Jewish immigrants were happy to have the opportunities ▶ that America offered.

Shabbat

My great-grandparents worked very hard every day. But they always stopped whatever they were doing before sundown on Friday nights to celebrate **Shabbat** (shuh-BOT), or the Sabbath. Shabbat celebrates the day after God finished creating the world. Jews believe that this is the day God rested, so we rest too. On the day before Shabbat, Grandma and her mother cooked a special meal for the family. Then, on Shabbat, they lit candles and said special prayers.

◀ My mother and I prepare food the night before Shabbat, just like this girl and her mother do.

13

Synagogue

My family still celebrates Jewish holidays the same way my grandma did when she was a kid. On every holiday, including Shabbat, we go to **synagogue** (SIN-uh-gog), or temple. Before we enter, my father puts a **yarmulke** (YAH-muh-kuh) on his head. He also wears a **talit** (ta-LEET) around his shoulders.

The **rabbi** (RAB-eye) guides everyone through the service, and the **cantor** (KAN-ter) leads all the songs.

Some Jewish services are said in English. Others are in Hebrew. ▶

Food

Grandma Lena loves to cook. She makes a special meal for every holiday. On Passover, she makes matzoh balls, which are round dumplings that go into chicken soup. On Hanukkah, she fries potato latkes, or pancakes. My grandma eats her latkes with sour cream. But I eat mine with applesauce. For Shabbat dinner, I always help her bake bread that looks like a fat braid. This bread is called challah.

◀ Challah has a yellow color because it is made with lots of eggs.

Israel

Israel is a small country in the Middle East. The official language of Israel is Hebrew. Israel is a very special place for Jews. Judaism started there thousands of years ago. Now Jewish people from all over the world go there to visit and pray at all the holy places. Israel is the one country in the world where Jews are not a minority.

Next year, my whole family is going to Israel for my sister's **Bat Mitzvah** (BOT MITZ-vuh).

Many Jews who visit Israel stop and pray at a special place called the Wailing Wall. ▶

Bat Mitzvah

When Jewish girls turn twelve, they have a Bat Mitzvah. When Jewish boys turn thirteen, they have a Bar Mitzvah. A Bat or Bar Mitzvah celebrates when a child becomes an adult according to the Jewish religion.

At her Bat Mitzvah, Lauren will read in Hebrew from the **Torah** (TOR-uh). Hebrew is the official language of all Jewish prayers. The Torah is very important to Jewish people because it includes all the teachings of Judaism. After Lauren's Bat Mitzvah service, we'll have a party for her.

◀ The Torah is a holy book. Each copy is handwritten and no one is allowed to touch the paper it is written on.

21

I Am Jewish American

My grandma says that the day she landed on Ellis Island was one of the scariest days of her life. She also thinks it was one of the best. She always tells us that one reason America is so special is that almost everyone is a minority of some kind. Americans can practice any religion and celebrate any traditions they want. Ask your parents or grandparents to tell you about some of the traditions in your family!

Glossary

Bar/Bat Mitzvah (BAR/BOT MITZ-vuh) A ceremony for a Jewish child when he or she turns twelve or thirteen.

cantor (KAN-ter) The person who leads the songs in synagogue.

immigrant (IM-uh-grent) A person who moves to a new country from another.

Judaism (JOO-day-izm) The religion that Jewish people follow.

minority (my-NOR-ih-tee) A group of people that is in some way different from most of the others around them.

rabbi (RAB-eye) The person who leads a service in synagogue.

Shabbat (shuh-BOT) The holy day of the week, starting Friday at sundown.

synagogue (SIN-uh-gog) A place where Jews go to pray together.

talit (ta-LEET) A long piece of cloth Jewish men put on their shoulders before they pray.

Torah (TOR-uh) A holy book for Jewish people. It is made up of the first five parts of the Bible.

tradition (truh-DISH-un) A way of doing something that is passed down from parent to child.

yarmulke (YAH-muh-kuh) A small, round cap worn on the top of a man's head.

Yiddish (YID-ish) A language created and used mostly by Jewish people.

23

Index

B
Bar Mitzvah, 21
Bat Mitzvah, 18, 21

C
cantor, 14
challah, 17

E
Ellis Island, 9, 10, 22

F
food, 6, 17

H
Hanukkah, 17

Hebrew, 18, 21

I
immigrants, 6, 9, 10

J
Judaism, 5

M
minority, 5, 18, 22

P
Passover, 17
prayers, 13, 21

R
rabbi, 14

S
Sabbath, 13
Shabbat, 13, 17
synagogue, 14

T
talit, 14
tenement, 10
Torah, 21
traditions, 6, 22

Y
yarmulke, 14
Yiddish, 9